They lived a long time ago in a time called the ice age.

For most of the year it was winter.
Oscar and Arabella liked the winter.

# Oscar and Arabella

## HOT HOT HOT

## by Neal Layton

Hodder
Children's
Books

A division of Hodder Headline Limited

Oscar was a woolly mammoth.
And so was Arabella.

They liked the snow, the ice and the freezing arctic winds.

But then summer
would arrive.

Oscar and Arabella
didn't like the
summer.

The sun would come out and melt all the ice and snow. Thousands of brightly coloured plants would appear from the ground, irritating their eyes and trunks.

ATCHOOO!

Then there were the insects...

And the dust.
And this summer was worse than most.

Buzzzzz

There didn't seem to be any end in sight, it just seemed to be getting hotter **and hotter** and hotter.

zzzzzzzzzzzzzzzzz

Oscar found a last piece
of ice behind a rock.

But as soon as he took it into the sun it disappeared.

And still it got **hotter.**

Arabella suggested that they seek shelter under the trees.

But none of the trees were big enough.
And it got hotter still.

Oscar thought he could
fan Arabella with a big leaf.

It kept Arabella cool but made him even hotter than he had been before.

Arabella suggested that if they jumped in the lake it might help cool them down a bit.

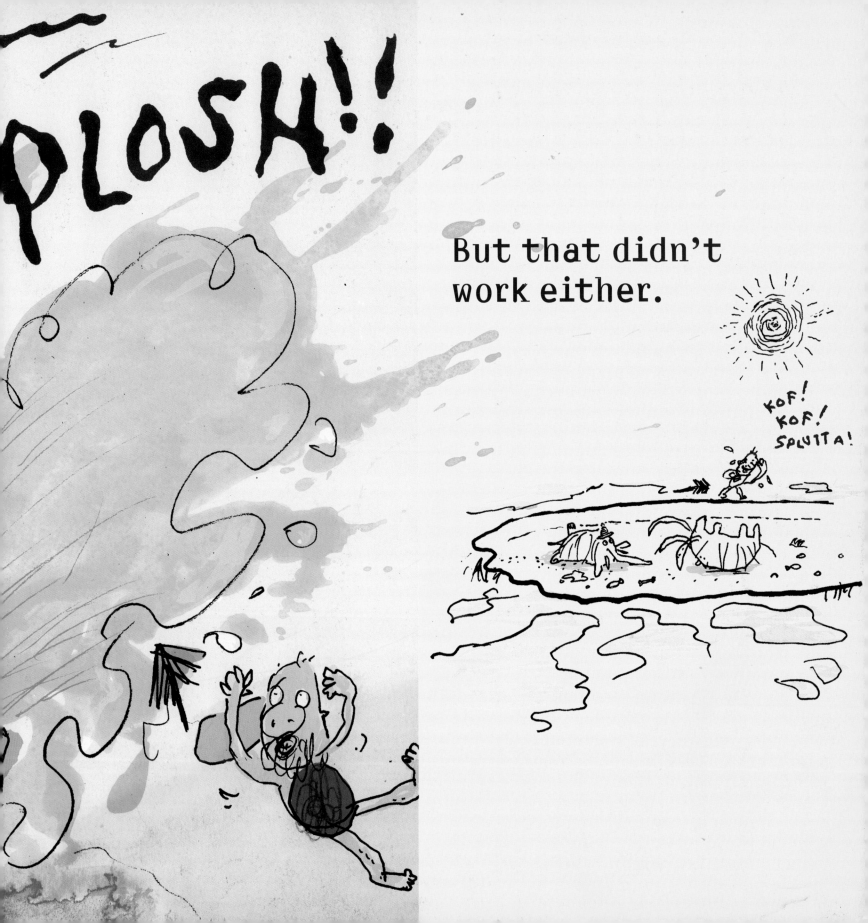

There was only one solution.

They would have to give each other a HAIR CUT!

It was drastic, but it worked.

At last they felt cool!

When all the other animals saw them, they decided to do the same.

The new fashion seemed to suit some animals more than others but at least now everybody was happy.

And thankfully,
summer never
lasts forever.

The world turned on
its axis, winter
set in once more...
and all the animals
grew back their
woolly coats.

Well almost all the animals...

# ICE AGE FACTS

There ~~has~~ actually has been more than one ice age. Oscar and Arabella would ~~have~~ have lived in the most recent one which ended about 10,000 years ago.

They had seasons in the **ICE AGE** much like ours though their summers would have been much shorter.

They probably didn't have combs, mirrors or scissors in the **ICE AGE** I made that bit up. They would have more likely cut their woolly coats with blunt stone axes.

Most scientists think there will be another **ICE AGE** in a few thousand thousand years...